CK JR
The
ACKYARDIGANS
nics Reading Program

ch, sh,
th, wh

Y0-CAW-161

Ghost Chase

by Sonia Sander

SCHOLASTIC INC.

New York   Toronto   London   Auckland   Sydney
Mexico City   New Delhi   Hong Kong   Buenos Aires

"Hi, I am Tyrone.
I am a ghost chaser.
When I hear a *whoo* sound,
I try to track it down."

"It is time to search
this ship and chase down
the bunch of ghosts
hiding there," said
Ghost Chaser Tyrone.

"Where are they?"
asked Ghost
Chaser Uniqua.
"I can hear them whisper
whoo, but I cannot
see them."

"Over there!" shouted Ghost Chaser Pablo. "They are in the shadows! How can we catch them?"

The three ghost chasers
tried to catch the ghosts
with big nets.
The ghosts just floated
right through the nets.

Then the ghosts turned
and chased after
the three ghost chasers.
"Where should we go?"
asked Ghost
Chaser Uniqua.

"Hide behind the mirror!" said Ghost Chaser Tyrone.

When the ghosts saw themselves in the mirror, they got scared.

They whirled around and dashed away in a flash.

"It worked! The ghosts
are gone and this place
is shipshape!"